THIS WALKER BOOK BELONGS TO:

_____

_____

_____

_____

WHERE'S MY

First published 2002 by Walker Books Ltd
87 Vauxhall Walk, London SE11 5HJ

10 9 8 7 6 5 4 3 2 1

© 2002 Susanna Gretz

This book has been typeset in
Stempel Schneidler

Printed in China

British Library Cataloguing in Publication Data:
a catalogue record for this book is available
from the British Library

ISBN 0-7445-8840-5 (hb)

ISBN 0-7445-9474-X (pb)

FUZZLE?

Search me!

How should I know?

Susanna Gretz

FALKIRK COUNCIL
LIBRARY SUPPORT
FOR SCHOOLS

WALKER BOOKS
AND SUBSIDIARIES
LONDON · BOSTON · SYDNEY

In Debbie's family, everyone is always losing things.
"Where are my pyjama bottoms?" says her dad.

"Where's my football kit?" says her big brother Dickie.
"Where's my lion mask?" says her little brother John.

"And where's Fuzzle, my best toy?" says Debbie.
Now, Debbie is always making toys:
there's Choccy, Snakey, Mrs Pillow and lots more.
But Fuzzle is new. "I just made him today ...
and now he's lost," Debbie tells Mum.

"And my glasses are lost too," grumbles Mum. She can hardly see to sort out the wash.

Debbie starts hunting.
There's no Fuzzle under the bed
but she does find Mum's glasses.

Mum is so happy!

There's no Fuzzle on the
coat rack but she does find
Dad's pyjama bottoms.

Dad is so happy!

There's no Fuzzle behind the sofa but she does find
Dickie's shorts, his socks and one of his football boots.

Dickie is so happy!

There's no Fuzzle in the cupboard but she does find John's lion mask.

John is so happy!

"I bet **YOU** took my Fuzzle, John," says Debbie.

"What's a Fuzzle?" asks John.

"Well, he's green..." says Debbie.

"Is this Fuzzle?" asks John.

"No, silly, that's my hat!"

"Is he fuzzy?" asks John.
"Very fuzzy," says Debbie,
as she burrows
in the dustbin.

"Is this Fuzzle?" asks John.

"No, silly, that's a mop!"

John keeps on guessing. "Is this Fuzzle?" he asks.

"No, no, no!" says Debbie. "That's Mum's cactus plant!"

She's not a bit happy.

By now it's getting late and everyone is yawning.
"Time for bed, little rabbits," says Mum.
"But I can't go to bed without my Fuzzle,"
   cries Debbie.

"Of course you can," says Dad,
"and tomorrow we'll find your puzzle."
"Not puzzle, **FUZZLE**!"
 roars Debbie …

and she throws herself on the floor.
"Good gravy!" says Mum.
The truth is, no one but Debbie
has the faintest idea what Fuzzle is.

"What does Fuzzle look like?" asks Dad.
"He's green," sniffs Debbie, "and fuzzy ...
and he has a stripy neck,
red and blue."

Mum has an idea.
"Is he dirty?" she asks.
"Well," says Debbie,
"maybe a little bit dirty."
"I bet I know," says John.
"I bet he's in the ...

WASH!"

Sure enough, there's Fuzzle …

and Dickie's football shirt, too.

Everyone settles
down to go to sleep.
But not for long…

"Where's my
cactus plant?"
says Mum.

"What's a Bunnyjumper?" asks John.

"I've no idea," says Dad, "but we'll find them all tomorrow."